This story is a work of fiction. Names, characters, businesses, places, events, and incidents are either the products of the author's imagination or used in a fictitious manner. Any resemblance to actual persons, living or dead, or actual events is purely coincidental.

Cover Art: HK Doodles

ISBN: 9798857738016

HK Doodles, Dunedin, FL

THE PECULIAR AFFLICTION
OF THOMAS WADE DUNCAN

A Dark Tale from
Kip Koelsch

For Jules.

ONE

"How came you here, soldier?"

I knew neither my place nor time. Many have been my experiences with thin, smoky mists and laying somewhat askew on my back—madly muddled have been those recollections. Where am I? When am I?

September? Wounded in the cornfield near Antietam Creek?

This mist smelled of smoke, but not that tangy, metallic variety leftover from the generous expenditure of gunpowder.

"How came you here, soldier?"

Surely that was an elderly woman's voice. Perhaps I was still lying on the battlefield? Perhaps a nurse discovered me?

No. The strong scent of saltwater was mixed with the misty smoke. I was no longer in that remote part of Maryland.

So where am I?

Something poked aggressively at my left shoulder, and I managed to open my eyes. The jabs had come from a walking cane, while the raspy inquiry appeared to originate from the grey-cloaked, elderly woman standing over me and wielding said stick.

"I asked, how did you come by Black Ledge Cove?"

Her cane tapped hard on my left foot—then flipped at the flap of shortened trouser leg on the right.

"Surely, someone facilitated your landing." She waved the cane at what I assumed were my belongings. "A trunk, satchel, a crutch. You did not swim to shore with those. You did not carry those here alone."

I could not yet speak. Consequently, I didn't reply. But I could hear her voice and now, the whispers of other women. At the blurry edge of my vision, I saw only smudgy, shadowy silhouettes.

"You do not belong here." The old woman repeatedly rapped on the hard, frozen ground to emphasize her point. "You do not belong here. No unscheduled ships ever stop at our island. It is known. We desire no visitors, and none are welcome."

In the silence that followed, I felt a small bottle in my coat pocket. The cork was loose enough that even my cold, addled hand managed its removal.

Shakily, I extracted the blessed elixir and brought it to my trembling lips. There was but half remaining, and after releasing a long sigh, the bottle slipped from my grasp. My heavy eyes closed, yet I could hear the shuffle of multiple footsteps.

"We can't leave him to freeze."

That was a new voice. Distinct. Even as the medicine gradually numbed my senses, I noted the difference in tone. Younger. Clearer. *Kinder?*

"He is of no use to us." The raspy, elderly voice was firm and stern. "Crippled in body."

As my consciousness slipped away, I could hear the cane send my small, empty bottle rolling along the cobblestones.

"Crippled in body," repeated the old woman before snidely adding, "Crippled in mind."

Crippled in mind? I was second in my class at Bowdoin. I had been a new but respected teacher before the war. That much I remember. Crippled in mind? I knew the accusation to be false, yet I could summon neither the will nor the voice to protest.

It was now muffled and distant, yet I still discerned the kinder voice pleading, "Regardless, ma'am — we must — "

"What we must do, Milly, is keep to our routine. I must open the library."

"Yes."

"It's nearly my time."

"Yes. Yes."

"And mine soon after."

Those were other softer voices. Mildly anxious. Clearly feminine. Distinctly reserved. I strained to listen, but the fog of ecstatic insensibility was becoming thicker.

"Ma'am, we must help him," said the younger woman — her tone somewhat confrontational.

"His kind does not belong here." Again, I could discern a firmness in the older woman's voice. "His kind is not—"

"Ma'am, we must help …"

Blissfully — finally — I slipped into the comfortable, full embrace of my narcotic abyss before I could hear the outcome of the women's debate.

***

Momentarily jostled back to semi-consciousness, I sensed that I was lying on my back, being haphazardly rocked back and forth. There was an accompaniment of faint voices and, again, a smoky mist. Where was I?

The back of a wagon being drawn through that lumpy Maryland cornfield to an improvised hospital in the rear?

No. I was alone on my back — not packed tight like sacks of flour with other wounded. And the murmurs were not the moans and repetitive, pleading prayers of those close to death.

In the longboat being rowed ashore from the *Alomsek?*

No. My head throbbed from the piercing clop of wheels on cobbles — not the rattle of the oars in the locks. The smoke wafting about my nose was from wood fires, not the coal-fed boiler of the steamship.

And the voices, faint to my ears, were feminine and humble—not the raucous mocking and masculine boasting of sailors.

Black Ledge Cove?

Yes. Yes, that must be it—Black Ledge Cove. The captain of the steamship. He gave orders to drop me there. The sailors. I heard them bellow with derisive laughter as they rowed and echoed his damning comments.

Cursed medicine. Weak, troubled soul. Cursed island. A fitting match. Get him off my ship! Row him ashore, now!

As the erratic rocking subsided, I drifted back into the cozy, protective haze of my intoxicated state. Still, I remembered and mouthed some of those disparaging and somewhat haunting words—*weak, cursed, fitting*—before losing consciousness.

TWO

"My leg! Don't take my leg!"

I was bound to my bed and shouted as I thrashed against those restraints.

"Don't take my leg! Don't take my leg!"

"Mr. Duncan, calm yourself!"

It was vaguely familiar; a young woman's voice.

"Nurse! Don't let them take my leg."

A gentle hand settled on my shoulder, and the same steady voice said, "You've already lost your leg, Mr. Duncan. Some months ago, from what we can tell."

I settled at the soft touch and reassuring tone of the young woman. My thrashing gave way to shivering, and I managed a weak whisper, "Perhaps. Yes. Some months ago. The war."

There was no strength or will to open my eyes. I could sense the dampness of my nightshirt and bedding as my chilled body shuddered.

"An … Ant … Antietam," I mumbled.

Cold sweat beaded on my forehead and slid down my stubbled cheeks. My breath quickened. The consequent pounding in my chest gave way to the throb running down what remained of my right leg.

"My medicine! Where is my medicine? Now! Fetch it for me!"

There was no reply, and the prickly burn—that persistent itch—allied with the relentless throbbing to amplify my torment.

"My medicine? I need my medicine! It's in my trunk, please. My medicine. Please!"

The hand on my shoulder grew firmer, and in that brief moment, I could hear a thump and shuffle along the wood flooring.

"You'll have none of that *medicine*. Now, Milly, tea."

It was a raspy, older woman's voice—authoritative. Through the thick tears in my eyes, I could see her hunched silhouette in the doorway—her wooden cane. I thought I had seen her before, but the image blurred as the hand on my shoulder disappeared, and my agony resumed.

"I'm afraid it's been locked away. Well-hidden."

"In my trunk, please! Please! Please—"

"You'll have none of that in your time here, Mr. Duncan." The old woman grew more insistent. "Tea, Milly."

My shouting devolved into child-like pleading. "Please … please … please …"

I barely noticed the exit of the younger, kinder woman. But I did hear the firm, close whisper of the elder.

"Your kind does not belong here. And, while you are here, you *will* do as I say."

I did not acknowledge the old woman's order or her leaving as my undivided attention returned to the tingling and throbbing of my leg.

***

"Tea, Mr. Duncan."

The caring, gentle voice was firm enough to wake me. And after forcing open my burning eyes, I could see her at the side of the bed — smooth, pale face framed by blond wisps peaking from beneath a plain, grey bonnet. A dull white apron wrapped itself around tightly enough to show some shape beneath her simple dress.

"The tea will help calm you. If you please …"

She bent closer and lifted the China cup to my trembling lips. I stared into her blue eyes as I sipped.

My nose instantly wrinkled, and I stuck out my tongue. "That's awful."

"It's not the best-tasting tea, but it will ease your — "

"Pain? No!" The burning desire for relief fueled my brief insistence. "My medicine. It … it is much more effective. Please! Please."

There was the hint of a smile—or was it a sneer—as she whispered, "Mrs. Dawes says you are to have none. It's an elixir most wicked. And … and she knows much of potions—both good and evil."

I sighed heavily but continued to take sips of the warm drink as offered. We exchanged no further words, and when the cup was empty, Milly left me alone—still lashed to my bed, my right leg still throbbing, and my eyes growing heavier.

***

"Time for more tea, Mr. Duncan."

I was awakened again by Milly's voice. This time, there was a light hand on my sweat-dampened shoulder.

"More? Al … al … already?" Chills raced across my moist skin, and my teeth chattered. "Wha … wha… what day …?" I could barely control my jaw to form the needed words. I fidgeted against my restraints. "I … I … the privy? Cha … chamber pot?"

I could feel the pressure building.

Milly set the cup on a side table and turned towards the open door. "Mrs. Dawes!"

The echoing shuffle and thump ended with the old woman standing in the doorway—glaring.

Milly turned, looked into my glassy eyes, and nodded.

I shivered and repeated my stammering. "I … I … the privy? Cha—?

"He is your charge now, girl. Help him with the chamber pot."

The younger woman's pale face flushed. For the first few difficult days, she had left the room while her mistress took care of bathing and changing me. For the last two—as my awareness improved slightly—I had spotted her observing from the hallway.

"His bindings, ma'am?" asked Milly.

"Loosened as needed—not removed. You've seen me do it, girl." She rapped her cane twice on the wood floor. "Now, see to it. Then, see that he drinks the tea. I must see to opening the library. All returns to normal today."

Mrs. Dawes left the room, and Milly proceeded to modestly assist me with my needs. Once I had finished, she removed the chamber pot and tightened my restraints. I looked up at her with pleading eyes.

Resting her hand on one of the straps, the young woman was apologetic. "Until the urges pass. I'm sorry. It's for your own good. Mrs. Dawes says it may be some days."

I moaned, but that evoked no commentary or extra pity from Milly. She simply retrieved the cup of tea, slid a chair close to the bed, and began administering small sips.

"How did you come by here, Mr. Duncan?"

I had no clear recollection. Since that dreadful day in the cornfield when the random bounce of an iron ball took off half of my right leg—since that moment the surgeon poured the first drops of sweet, oblivious relief into my mouth—my memories were mere shadows of scenes. Chaotic flashes. Unreliable.

My answer would have to wait—perhaps it would never come. Instead, I asked my own question, "Where is *here*?"

"Very well." Milly gave me another sip of tea. "Black Ledge Cove. Our village is on a small island well to the north of Cape Ann. Mariners used to call it Black Ledge Rock."

"Used to?" I was confused. "And now?"

Milly sighed, tipped another sip of tea over my lips, and set the cup on the side table. She looked at her hands—now folded and fiddling in her lap.

"Some years ago, they called it *that cursed island, Witches Rock*. These days, most don't call it anything at all. They stay away. I understand it's a black mark on the newer charts. None stops here. Seaman up and down the coast, they all know never to drop anchor or come ashore. Never. We were all quite taken aback to see you lying near the pier that morning. Surprised. Frightened, at first."

My eyes went wide at one phrase—*Witches Rock?* I fixated on that name while bits and pieces of Milly's ramblings passed through the still-persistent mists of my mind.

"I don't understand." I shook my still feverish head slightly. "Witches Rock?"

Through the prolonged silence, through the nearly ever-present tears in my eyes, I could see Milly thinking—mulling. But she never answered that question or expanded beyond her original narrative, and I had no desire or energy to pursue the obviously avoided inquiry further. Instead, I filed away the thought and, somewhat more clear-headed asked another question.

"What about *Mr.* Dawes? Is he at sea? Joined the fight in the South?"

There was another pause—a hush over the room—and I thought I had perhaps overstepped my bounds. I started to apologize, "I'm sorry—"

"He's dead. Long dead." Milly didn't elaborate. She retrieved the teacup and changed the subject. "You need to finish this, and I need to go about my daily duties."

"So, Mrs. Dawes is the Widow Dawes?"

Again, silence.

I was eager for more information. In my frustration, I closed my mouth to reject the offered tea, and it spilled down my unshaven chin and onto my nightshirt.

"Childish man! We were just fine without—" Milly stopped herself, took a deep breath, and continued to scold me—albeit a bit more calmly. "I don't have time for this—to bathe you today, Mr. Duncan. Finish drinking so that I can get to my chores. I must tend to my work. Please."

There was an air of urgency—a tinge of fear—to her latter words, and I acquiesced. After finishing the tea, she scurried for the door. I raised my voice above the clomp of her footsteps and, "Thank you. Perhaps tomorrow."

THREE

Another day passed with no conversation from Milly or the widow — and another after that. Finally, following my usual morning tea, the two women returned to my room, pulled two chairs close to the bedside, and sat.

The older woman spoke first. "Thomas Wade Duncan."

"Yes, ma'am." I could feel the warmth well up and spread through my body — and the perspiration forming on my brow. "Thomas."

"Mr. Duncan, I am Ann Holland Dawes — mistress of this household and leader of our small village."

"Librarian," I quipped — surprised at my mind's quicker reaction.

"Indeed." She glared at Milly and then returned her eyes to mine. "I can only assume that your affliction — *addiction* — affected your onboard behavior in a most heinous way. You became a *persona non grata* on whatever ship you sailed."

"Steamed, I believe." Yes, some thoughts were becoming a little clearer. "I distinctly remember the scent of coal smo—"

The widow held up a hand, and I stopped. She continued, "It is known by all those who ply nearby waters — whalers, fishermen, schooners, steamships, sailors. It is known in ports up and down the east coast that no one is allowed to land here. Merchants are not welcome. Curiosity seekers are not welcome." There was a pause and possibly a brief crack in her stoicism before she emphatically stated, "The *sick* are not welcome."

"And I am sick."

"You are," replied Mrs. Dawes as she glanced at Milly. "And I suspect your sickness caused that steamship captain and his crew to ignore those warnings and maroon you and your belongings on our shore."

I closed my eyes. The *Alomsek.* Baltimore. How did I get to Baltimore? How did my trunk and satchel get to that port? How had I purchased my trunk? Had I purchased it? What had I bartered for the case of laudanum I'd smuggled onboard in my luggage? I could not yet remember those details. But I *was* beginning to recall the devolution of my voyage — from the initial hazy bliss to the hysterical possession of paranoia. I could see them staring at my leg. A mild offense. The children scurried away—frightened. The men? Most pointed and shook their heads. Some averted their eyes after a furtive glance. The bawdier ones grabbed their crotches and laughed. The ladies? Honestly, I remember only one. Cynthia? No. She just had the look of my beloved—smiled like my fiancée. But she … her … her smile turned to a frown?

"Mr. Duncan?" It was Milly's softer voice.

I could not answer—frozen by the memory of that moment on the *Alomsek*. I had hobbled along the rail and approached my Cynthia—put my hands on hers. She recoiled. I did not handle the rejection well. I did not. The rage. Yes. I could feel my fury pressing outward. I stumbled back on the icy deck and tumbled into a heap. I could hear the distant laughter. Then, my beloved put one foot up on the railing and started to climb …

"No!"

I flopped toward her, shouted again, and levered myself upright. Just as I put my hands on her, a nearby crewman wrestled us both to the deck. There, even through bleary eyes, I could see that the female face next to mine was not hers.

"Cynthia?"

As I was dragged away in a muddled cacophony of shouts and snickers—through the fog of my intoxication—I could see a well-dressed man embracing and calming the woman.

"It was not Cynthia." I grinned. "It wasn't her … it wasn't her … Cynthia … it wasn't you …"

I lay in the bed muttering—though in my mind I was elsewhere—and nowhere.

"Perhaps, Mr. Duncan is not quite ready, Milly." The older woman leaned on her cane and started to stand. "Perhaps tomorrow."

"Yes, ma'am." Milly also stood. Her blue eyes looked on me with pity. "I think you may be right."

"Of course, I'm right, girl." Mrs. Dawes shuffled to the door. "Come now, get Mr. Duncan more tea."

The gist of their discussion was lost on me — as I was still back on board the *Alomsek* and awash in those dreadful memories. All I could think about was getting my sweating hands — my now trembling lips — on another bottle of opium. All I could think about was blissful escape.

FOUR

I have no idea how many more days I lay restrained in that room. While the sweats, chills, and throbbing in my leg eventually decreased, I still struggled with my memories. I do know the daily doses of tea continued. Milly's assistance with the chamber pot continued. The addition of porridge and, eventually, a hearty stew to my diet was welcome—for both the sustenance and the routine that seemed to finally assist with measuring the passage of time.

This morning, the two women again sat before me.

"You will be with us until the spring supply ship arrives," chirped Milly.

I tilted my head and squinted at the young woman. She had told me that no ships landed at Black Ledge Cove. "Ship?"

Mrs. Dawes scowled and answered, "A lone ship arrives quarterly—on the solstices and equinoxes. The next comes in March. We will arrange your passage on that ship."

"When ... when ..." I could not recall when I had boarded the *Alomsek*. I knew the battle in the cornfield had been in September, but all that followed the field hospital was a jumble. "When did I arrive?"

"December 24. Three days after the arrival of our last supply ship. We were returning to the village proper after doing some early morning work in one of our warehouses when we discovered you near the pier."

Foggy images and muffled voices from that morning wafted through my mind. Warehouse work? Had I only heard female voices that morning? Seen female silhouettes? Was this truly an island of witches? A coven?

"As I said, until the spring equinox, we think it best that you be given a role in our community. Idle hands, an idle mind—those will only lead you back to self-destruction."

"Before the war, I was a teacher, ma'am. Perhaps the children would benefit—"

"We have no children here." The old woman's reply was terse, and she did not elaborate.

I glanced at Milly, but her head was down—her eyes closed.

"You've been in bed for over a week. You've been addled by that poison for much longer. It will take some time to regain your strength and mobility.

Milly will assist you with daily exercises until you can help tend to the sheep in their winter barn."

"I'm not averse to manual labor, ma'am, but the library …" I grinned before continuing, "Perhaps that would be a better fit for a teacher."

"No." Her reply was not quite a shout—but nearly so. "You're not to set foot in the library—ever."

Again, I looked toward Milly. Again, her head was down, and her eyes closed. Subservient.

"I know little of sheep, ma'am. But books …"

Honestly, I knew nothing of sheep. And while at Bowdoin, I knew the placement of every volume within the college's library.

"Yes, I've looked through your books—an eclectic assortment."

"Perhaps I could donate them to your collection and then—"

"I'll have no further talk of the library. You are an unwelcome guest here, Mr. Duncan. You would be wise to accept my rules and appreciate our hospitality." With the aid of her cane, Mrs. Dawes stood. "Now, Milly, fetch Mr. Duncan's morning tea and porridge. After he has eaten, remove his restraints and begin his exercises."

The younger woman stood and left the room.

"Good day, Mr. Duncan." she glared and nodded before turning towards the door.

"My books, Mrs. Dawes?"

She paused but did not turn. "Yes?"

"May I at least have access to my books?"

"Milly will retrieve the trunk for you. Now, good day."

As the older woman's shuffle and clomp faded, my thoughts shifted to reading—to my books. My books? Yes, some were mine—*Moby Dick*, Homer's *Odyssey* and *Iliad*, *Leaves of Grass*, *Walden*, a collection of essays by Emerson. The handful I'd managed to keep in my rucksack from the outset of my mustering. The others in my trunk? I'd collected those from a pile at the field hospital. They were unclaimed. Left by dead men I knew and some I didn't.

FIVE

"This is a different tea." I grinned as a pleasing flavor lingered in my mouth.

"It is." Milly guided my now unbound hand as I weakly raised the cup to my lips again.

After taking a longer sip, I noted, "A most pleasant change."

"The other mixture was to ease the effects of no longer habitually ingesting that bottled poison. I'm still learning the proper methods of combination and brewing and their applications, but this is similar to a tea given to women following childbirth."

My eyes went wide, and Milly could see the immediacy of my concern. It was the first time I sensed the hint of a laugh from the young woman. She shook her head. "It's been modified according to one of the old books—Proctor and Basset. And according to Mrs. Dawes, will aid in returning your vitality."

"As you say."

I finished the tea, and Milly pulled back the heavy down comforter.

"Let's start with sitting at the edge of the bed."

"Good."

After shifting my body, I was winded but felt strong enough to do more. I nodded toward my wooden crutch. It had first appeared in the room that morning. "For me?"

"Yes." Milly retrieved the crutch.

With one hand on the thick stick and my left foot firmly planted on the floor, I stood—and sat. I repeated the motion twenty-four times. After standing for the twenty-fifth, I asked, "May I rest by the window for a few moments?"

"Of course—if you believe you are up to a few steps."

I nodded.

One by one, Milly slid two chairs across the wooden floor. Then, she pulled the heavy winter draperies aside. A dull light filled the room—not the glow of the full sun on a crisp, clear morning.

Slipping the crutch under my right arm, I took five tentative steps toward the window. Milly guided me into the chair.

"Thank you."

I beheld the outside. Occasional banks of fog rushed past the frosty glass. Beyond, between the sparse, bare trees and grey, weather-worn buildings, gusts of wind kicked up plumes of snowflakes from the frozen ground. I could feel my body relax, and I took a deep breath. The harsh winter scene was bleak yet exhilarating—a welcome change from the claustrophobia of the small room and my own mind. I grinned. "Thank you, Milly."

"You're welcome, Mr. Duncan."

"Thomas."

"Mrs. Dawes would not approve."

"Well, Mrs. Dawes is already at the library, is she not?"

"She—"

"People!" I raised my right hand and pointed. Since the day of my arrival, I had not seen a soul save Milly and Mrs. Dawes—and on that blur of a morning, there had been only the vague, shadowy shapes of other women. "Apologies, Milly. But, going in and out of that building. A woman just left, and another entered immediately."

"The library."

The woman who had just left passed close to the window as she walked. I focused on her astonishing face. The distant eyes. The smile. That smile. A simple bliss.

"I should like to sit here a bit."

"I'd prefer if we got you back into bed, Mr. Duncan. A fall would be a setback with consequences. And Mrs. Dawes would—"

I sighed. "I promise to sit until you return to assist me. Please, it's been so long since I've seen more than the inside of this room."

"Very well," Milly stood and slid her chair to the side. "I'll return when I've completed my chores. At most an hour. Then, no discussion—back to bed."

"Agreed."

She left the room, and I returned my eyes to the outside—to the library—and waited.

***

"Only the village's women use the library?"

Milly had completed her work and returned to assist me back to bed. When she didn't answer immediately, I rephrased my query. "None of the men use the library?"

Standing behind the other chair, she looked down at the empty seat and whispered, "There are no men in Black Ledge Cove, Mr. Duncan."

The answer was not what I had expected. And truth be told, I was a bit astonished. Still, I continued to seek answers. "Out at sea?"

"You wouldn't ask that question if you had been clear-minded enough to see the state of our harbor when you were rowed ashore. The decrepit, old pier is unsafe to traverse. The eerie hulks and masts of three half-sunken whalers make the cove nearly unnavigable. The rotting fishing skiffs onshore greatly outnumber our few sea-worthy ones."

I sighed. "Off to the war then?"

Milly finally turned her eyes to me. I could not imagine her face any paler, yet it was.

"No," she answered—offering nothing more—though I could see her gaze drift to a distant, troubling place and time. I did not press but rather gripped my crutch and stood.

It was enough to break her trance. "Let me help you."

The young woman moved to my left side and placed her right hand in the middle of my back. Once I was safely returned to bed, and the comforter pulled high, Milly slid one of the chairs closer and firmly whispered, "You mustn't repeat any of this to Mrs. Dawes—ever. Never."

I nodded, but she didn't see it. Instead, she had walked back to the window. My best guess was that she was surveying the library—looking for her mistress. After closing the heavy drapes—again darkening the room—she turned back and moved the chair even closer to my bedside.

"All the men left years ago," she whispered. Her eyes darted to the doorway and back to me.

"No men *and* no children?" I remembered an earlier conversation with Milly and Mrs. Dawes.

The young woman took a deep breath but did not answer. She closed her eyes and exhaled.

"Okay." I decided to keep to our original topic. "How long ago did the men leave?"

Milly shrugged and shook her head.

"Why? Why did the men leave?"

"The library." Again, her voice was a whisper. Again, her eyes searched the doorway.

"The library?" I sat up a bit straighter in bed and nodded. "Why the library?"

Milly stood and rushed to the window. "I can't, Mr. Duncan." She pulled aside the heavy drape just enough to peek outside. "It's nearly midday. I must finish preparing the midday meal. Mrs. Dawes, she …"

"Another time." I sighed and licked my lips. "Perhaps tomorrow while I am doing my exercises."

"Perhaps." Her accompanying nod was barely noticeable as she ran out of the room.

My curiosity did not want to wait until tomorrow. But I also did not want to press my kind caretaker or cause trouble for her with Mrs. Dawes. After all, I *was* their unwanted and unwelcome guest. Still, the *library*?

SIX

My question was not addressed the next day — or the next. It was nearly a week before I was able to tactfully ask Milly about the men who had once inhabited the village. It was my first excursion out of the house — albeit a short walk to the outdoor privy. Upon our return, I suggested sitting on the porch — to take advantage of the rare sunshine and warmth of the winter day.

She acquiesced, and as we sat on the frosted porch bench, I noticed a smile flash over Milly's face.

"What is it?" I asked as I also grinned.

"Mr. Duncan, you are the first man I've seen since I was a very young girl — up close, anyway." I noted that Milly's cheeks were reddened by more than the cold breeze. "Mrs. Dawes has warned me about men — and about you in particular."

"Me? In particular?"

"She is quite convinced that your addiction has given you exceptional powers of persuasion."

"Yet she leaves you alone to tend to me."

"She's raised me since my father left with the others. She is sometimes harsh, but she does entrust me with many responsibilities." Her smile dissolved as she continued, "Oh, I'm not perfect. No angels here in Black Ledge Cove. I have caught glimpses of the merchant sailors who row our provisions ashore each quarter. Typically, a rough lot. But some … one or two maybe … were as fine-looking as you."

I started to chuckle but held back. "I assure you—I have no nefarious intentions. I'm no threat to you." I thought about taking her hands in mine— reassuring her; I thought of telling her of my fiancée— of my aching and conflicted heart. I wanted to tell her that I was too broken to love anyone. But I did not.

The young woman looked away and sighed. "I barely remember any of the men from the village— even my own father. Mrs. Dawes assures me I am better off. My father, he …"

With her lost in thought, yet seemingly opening up to me, I asked, "Your father, the other men, Milly— and the children—what happened to them all?"

"Mr. Dawes," she replied before pausing. I could see tears welling up in Milly's blue eyes. "It was so long ago, and I was but a little girl. I knew Rebecca, but she was years older than I."

"Rebecca?"

"The Dawes's daughter." Milly lifted her head and took in the scene before her—the other houses, the road to the waterfront. "They were the wealthiest family in Black Ledge Cove. Mr. Dawes owned the whaling ships and the warehouses — the largest flock of sheep and the icehouse. He had taken Rebecca to Boston for her thirteenth birthday. When they returned …"

Tears ran down Milly's red cheeks.

I did not press. I waited.

"Scarlet fever took all the children — save me."

"Why you?" I shifted on the bench and turned to Milly. "How?"

"Mrs. Dawes was the village midwife. The closest thing we had to a physician at the time. She consulted all the old books and tried many mixtures — poultices and elixirs. None cured the fever. None cured the children — my sister and Rebecca. All were lost."

"Save you."

Milly nodded. "The last tonic Mrs. Dawes mixed broke my fever. I survived. Yes. But the other children … all dead."

"That's terrible to be —"

"The men …" She continued as though I hadn't begun speaking. I stayed silent. "They blamed Mr. Dawes for bringing back the fever. My father claimed he got it out of him — that Mr. Dawes knew there was an epidemic in Boston and still traveled there and back with Rebecca. My father … the other men … they …"

Milly looked up at the sun, and her glistening eyes went wide. "We've sat here too long. I've told you too much. We must —"

I put my closest hand firmly on the young woman's shoulder to keep her from standing.

"Please, Milly—I need to know."

She continued as though she had never stopped. "They … they had no proper trial. There was a huge oak tree where the library now stands. Part of the Dawes property. They hung him from that tree. Mr. Dawes—they hung him until he was dead."

"And the men fled the island after that?"

"No."

"No?"

"No." Milly fidgeted on the bench. "The library drove them away—away from their wives, their homes, their village."

"The library?"

Milly again looked at the sun. "I must prepare the midday meal, Mr. Duncan. We can—"

"Please, I—"

"After our meal. When Mrs. Dawes returns to the library." Milly stood and stepped towards the door. "After our meal."

***

Our lunch was nearly silent. Finally, the Widow Dawes inquired about the outcome of my first foray outdoors and, upon learning of my success, decided that I would start working with the sheep in the winter barn the following day.

As we finished the meal, the old matriarch said, "Milly, I'll need your assistance in the library following the clearing and washing of the dishes."

"Yes, mistress."

I said nothing and sighed. Knowing my continuing conversation with the younger woman would again be delayed, I stood and relegated myself to my room. A few days ago, Milly had dragged my trunk against the wall near the window — but I had yet to open it. I had spent those intervening days trying to remember what it contained. Books, for sure — but what else? Letters from Cynthia? A photograph? My journal? My uniform? Some additional items of clothing? A lone, unnoticed bottle of medicine?

Which of those items — and the associated, though bleary, memories — had kept me from opening the trunk? I sat in one of the chairs by the window and stared out as thin, gray clouds settled over the island and hid the sun. A few minutes later, my temporary trance was broken as I spotted Mrs. Dawes entering the library. Another woman quickly appeared and followed her through the door.

I sighed, scooted my chair a few inches closer to the trunk, and opened it. It was obvious that Mrs. Dawes and Milly had sorted through and straightened the belongings in my chest when they had removed the small crate of laudanum. My books were stacked in two piles on the left side. Clothing was carefully folded on the right. The neatly bundled letters were set on top of my uniform jacket. I hadn't left them wrapped in that ribbon. Or had I? My last encounters with the trunk and its contents had been on board the *Alomsek* — at that time, I was not of sound mind.

I did not immediately spy my journal. Had it even been packed in my haste to flee Baltimore? Yes, I'm sure of it. Am I? What else seemed to be missing?

My eyes were fixated on the bundle of letters. The envelope on top was addressed by Cynthia's hand. Was it her troubling last letter? Sweat beaded on, then ran down my back as I tried to reread her words in my mind. Bits and pieces—my thoughts only held a few phrases and sentences. But one part stood out:

If I can't have you, I can't go on.

In a moment of self-loathing—a day of worthless intoxication in some squalid Baltimore rooming house—I had sent her a letter breaking our engagement. I begged her to move on—to find a *whole man* to share her life. Her letter, her response, chilled me enough to recant. I quickly penned two letters. Or had they been telegrams? Did I spare the money to send one to her father and one to her?

I kicked at the trunk with my left leg and nearly toppled over from the impact. After righting myself on the chair, I focused and remembered. Her father had sent funds to purchase my passage on the *Alomsek*. I had been on my way to Brunswick—to Cynthia— when I'd been marooned on the shores of Black Ledge Cove due to my abhorrent behavior.

How long would she wait? Would she wait? Did she even know to expect me?

Out of the corner of my eye, I spotted a woman leaving the library. As she disappeared into the thickening fog, Milly emerged from the mist and guided someone else up the steps and through the door of that forbidden building.

My hope was that Cynthia would wait for me until the spring—when I could find passage on another ship—when I could leave this dour place. Her father had received my letter—or telegram--so I was fairly certain he had shared the news of my eventual arrival.

That mildly comforting thought quieted my spinning mind for the moment, and I reached toward the stacks of books in my trunk. I pulled the third edition of Whitman's *Leaves of Grass* from the closest pile. Cynthia was enamored with the recent emergence of a truly American literature, and this book of poetry had been a parting gift as I headed off to the war.

I began by silently reading *Song of Myself*—absorbed into the rhythm and passion of Whitman's words. The last two stanzas, I whispered aloud:

> *You will hardly know who I am or what I mean,*
> *But I shall be good health to you nevertheless,*
> *And filter and fibre your blood.*

> *Failing to fetch me at first keep encouraged,*
> *Missing me one place search another,*
> *I stop somewhere waiting for you.*

I was rapt—drawn into the words, drawn into wonderful memories of my beloved. Our shared love of learning, languages—of words. But those last lines

41

twisted in and gnawed at my mind. Was Cynthia waiting for me? Did she know I was onboard the *Alomsek*? Had I sent a telegram of confirmation to her or her father? Or had I traded my first-class ticket for a berth in steerage and a few additional bottles of laudanum? I could not recall.

I returned to Whitman, thumbed through the pages, and a lock of ash brown hair fell at my feet. After retrieving the lock, I set it back into the pages at the beginning of *I Sing the Body Electric*. I carefully balanced the book to not drop the hair again and began reading aloud:

> *I sing the body electric,*
> *The armies of those I love engirth me and I*
> *engirth them,*
> *They will not let me off till I go with them,*
> *respond to them,*
> *And discorrupt them, and charge them full*
> *with the charge of the soul …*

Again, I was transported by the deep emotion and power of the words, which was reflected in my enthusiastic recitation. Each stanza took me further from my previously unanswered questions and their consequent insecurities.

> *O I say these are not the parts and poems of*
> *the body only, but of the soul,*
> *O I say now these are the soul!*

A gasp and deep exhale quickly turned my head to the door. So lost in the poetry had I been that I did not hear the approach of Milly. Now, she stood there — wide-eyed and red-faced.

"How …" I stammered a little. Previously, I had only read with comparable passion for my beloved. "How long have you been listening?"

She cleared her throat and closed her eyes before passionately whispering:

> *If anything is sacred the human body is sacred. And the glory and sweet of a man is the token of manhood untainted. And in man or woman a clean, strong, firm-fibred body, is more beautiful than the most beautiful face. Have you seen the fool that corrupted his own live body? Or the fool that corrupted her own live body?*

"You have quite a memory." I was taken aback. The surprising young woman had recited a portion of the previous stanza without error. I carefully closed the book and set it back in the trunk.

"I've read Mr. Whitman many times before. One of my favorites." Bashfully, she looked at her feet. "But I've never heard it read aloud."

"I hope my reading was to your liking."

Milly looked up wide-eyed and smiling.

"Is it shelved in the library?" I asked.

"No, in the basement — with Mrs. Dawes's other books."

"Books that aren't in the library?"

"Yes." Milly stepped closer to my chair. She bent over and whispered, "Books she says shouldn't be spoken of with common people — unenlightened folk."

"And that doesn't include you?" As I asked my question, she stepped back and behind the other chair.

"Mrs. Dawes has looked after my schooling and training since I was a girl."

"Training? As a housemaid? A midwife?"

"Yes."

I could see I would get no elaboration from Milly, so I turned and closed the lid on my trunk. The stack of letters again caught my eye, and I lingered with my head turned away. I heard the young woman step towards the door and pause.

"I'll make your afternoon tea, Mr. Duncan."

Her steps faded down the hallway, and I flipped open my chest. Cynthia? I reached for the bundle of letters and paused — my attention redirected by the dark shape of another woman leaving the library. That place. I needed to know more about that place.

SEVEN

The following morning, I donned my army-issue overcoat, and Milly led me to the winter barn. One of the other women had already raked out and laid fresh hay in the pens. I was to feed and water the sheep.

It was relatively easy work, and I completed my task within the hour. My strength and stamina had returned, and I was only limited by my skill—which was increasing—using my crutch. I had received no further instructions from Milly and therefore decided it was time for me to revisit the waterfront where the crew of the *Alomsek* had left me—and maybe explore the village proper upon my return up the hill.

Much was as Milly had described. The decrepit pier had few intact planks and too many gaps for me to attempt further exploration--even if there had been no slick, frozen coating. Farther out, protruding from the pulsing, grey slush and patchy harbor ice, I could see the masts and top rails of three large ships—Mr. Dawes's whalers. Neglected rigging dangled from the yardarms and, glazed with rime ice, creaked and cracked in the breeze. Turning and gazing upon the curving shoreline, I shook my head—several rotted fishing skiffs lay on the smooth, fist-sized stones.

I walked along the cobbled street—past several large, padlocked warehouses. Beyond the last was what remained of the local try-works—broken down brick furnaces and large iron cauldrons for processing whale blubber. The road ended there, and I turned around. Peeking into the last of the warehouses—the only one with windows--I did note two fine fishing skiffs, some well-maintained nets, and a few functional lobster traps. In warmer weather, the women must have used those to supplement their foodstuffs.

Starting back up the hill, I paused. The clouds blew clear for a moment, and I could take in the bulk of the village—over a dozen homes sitting in a mostly flat valley between two much higher, rocky prominences. The dreary, dull overtones of the hamlet were due to more than the weathered wood of the houses, the sparse, bare trees, and the nearly ever-present fog—the backdrop of steep and dominant cliffs was distinctly dark.

With the next frigid wind gust, the fog rolled in thick and again obscured my view. Hence, I began walking—though my head and gaze were still inclined toward those imposing black cliffs. Just two steps in, the tip of my crutch slipped on a small patch of ice beneath the snow. I landed roughly on the hard, cobbled ground. The stump of my right leg took the brunt of my fall, and bolts of pain shot up and through the rest of my body.

"Mr. Duncan!"

I had been on the ground but for a moment. The shout I heard was from Milly. She must have gone to the barn to check my progress, noticed my absence, and begun searching.

"My leg!" I fumbled with the crutch and grabbed at my stump—writhing on the slick, frozen stones. "Help me, Milly!"

It was a familiar pain—like I had landed on shards of broken glass. I'd felt it before—when I was first issued a crutch, when I failed and repeatedly fell when I was convalescing in Washington City. I also recalled what had taken away that pain—that little magic bottle.

"Let me take you home." Milly snatched away my crutch and offered her gloved hand. I grasped her forearm and braced my left foot in the crook between two cobbles. "Up!" she said firmly.

"Thank you," I whispered—managing to reply through my clenched teeth and quivering lips.

"Let's get you back into bed where I can get a look at and tend to your leg."

I said nothing more on our walk back to the Dawes house. Milly supported one side while I still used my crutch. I was focused on carefully placing my foot and the tip of the stick. Still, I couldn't help noticing another woman leaving the library as we approached our destination. She passed us on the path, and I saw her face — distant yet sparkling eyes, a slight smile. Contentment? There was no acknowledgment as we passed. I was unsure if she even saw us.

***

I barely remember entering the house, Milly helping me into bed, taking off my trousers, and treating my bleeding stump. The pain and the dark recollections associated with the loss of my leg were that powerful — the blissful memory of my chosen medicine returned and clouded my mind. Apparently, that wicked elixir had not completely lost its powers of seduction.

"Tea, Mr. Duncan?"

Startled by the once familiar voice, it felt like I had regressed weeks. As the shivering increased, I knew I had no choice but to accept the warm tonic. Faintly, I answered, "Yes, please."

With small, guided sips, I finished the tea. Milly left me alone after drawing the heavy draperies over the window. I closed my teary eyes, and gradually, the waves of sharp pain subsided. The nearly forgotten throb and itch returned — though with less intensity. I was certain a few sips of laudanum would make it go away — make it all go away. The mere thought of the effects of that precious medicine seemed to relax first my legs, then my torso and arms, my neck, and finally my face.

Face? My now somewhat muddled mind drifted to the woman we'd passed on the path—her expression. An eerie, hypnotic contentment. Had I seen that look before? Had I seen it in the cracked mirror of that Baltimore rooming house?

EIGHT

"Thank you again for your help yesterday." I was sitting in my chair by the window — contemplating my open trunk — when Milly entered the room. I turned and continued in a whisper. "I assume you told Mrs. Dawes nothing of my fall?"

"No. She would have scolded you at breakfast if I had." Milly moved closer to where I was sitting. She also whispered, "You did an admirable job coming and going from the table this morning. She suspects nothing — said nothing to me. The pain has subsided?"

"Your tea was most helpful."

"And the bleeding has stopped?"

I nodded. The talented young woman had made a soothing poultice that seemed to quickly clot and heal my abrasions.

"So …?"

She moved to where my heavy coat hung on a peg and retrieved the garment.

"So, I should tend to the sheep."

She grinned shyly and replied, "Yes, the sheep."

I stood, and she helped me into my multi-layered army overcoat. She looked at the gold buttons and then the bundle of letters in the still-open trunk.

"Why did you leave her for the war?"

I leaned on my crutch and slowly buttoned the coat. When I finished, I looked at the door and said, "I should tend to the sheep."

Milly's face went blank, and she handed me a wool cap. "Hard to believe, but it is colder this morning."

"Thank you." I donned the hat, stepped toward the door, and paused. "Will you have time for some Whitman this afternoon?"

I noted the slightest of glances toward my open trunk, and she answered, "Perhaps something else from your collection."

Nodding, I replied, "Very well. An essay from Emerson, maybe. After the midday meal then."

"Yes. I'd like that." Milly left the room, and I could hear her steps fade into the pantry.

Crutch in place, I shuffled down the hallway to the front door. I recall hesitating. Had the pause been necessary to steel myself for the cold, damp air or the impending stench of the winter barn? No. I'd grown used to both. In truth, I remember being momentarily overwhelmed by the genuine kindness of an exceptional young woman.

***

I waited in my room following the midday meal. I flipped through Emerson from my chair, but nothing struck my fancy. I sat the book on the other chair and gazed into my trunk at the bundle of letters. I ran a finger over the ribbon that bound them together and along the edge of the top envelope.

My leaving for the war—delaying our wedding to join the army—had been a mutual decision. Cynthia had been as opposed to slavery as I. As ardent abolitionists, we agreed it was worth the risk. But as I sat in my room, re-reading her last letter, I could not help but doubt our youthful idealism.

If I can't have you, I can't go on. My heartbreak must be brought to an end.

I held the letter to my nose and inhaled the slightest hint of perfume. Tears welled in my eyes. I had no word from my beloved—nothing followed the desperate letter I posted after receiving this threat to end her life. Letter? Or was it a telegram? I truly could not recall if I sent anything to her at all. Had I only contacted her father? So much of that time in Baltimore was lost in a medicinal blur. Surely, she was well—waiting for me at home.

"Mr. Duncan." I could hear the young woman step into my room.

As I turned, eyes red and tears streaking my cheeks, she gasped. "Are you ailing? Has the pain--?"

53

"My humble apologies, Milly." I glanced at the copy of Emerson's essays I had set on the other chair — then, to the letter in my trembling hand. "I'm going to forego reading with you this afternoon."

"Is there anything — ?"

"Tea, please."

While Milly brewed the tea, my eyes lifted and lost themselves in the fog drifting before the library and through the other buildings of the village. I focused on the library. Perhaps thinking about that nagging mystery would distract my mind — push the memories back into a safe place. Or perhaps some actual action would be the remedy?

Yes. Action! Gripping my crutch, I levered myself up and hobbled to the door. Listening intently, I could hear Milly still at work in the kitchen. Determined, I donned my greatcoat and quietly made for the front door.

***

"I said never, Mr. Duncan!" The bulging, demonic eyes of Mrs. Dawes nearly popped out of their wrinkled, sunken sockets as she stood. Her black shadow grew on the wall of books behind her — doubling her small, hunched frame into a more imposing figure. Her usual rasp took on a deeper, sinister tone. "Leave at once!"

Instead, I took two steps forward, and the library door closed behind me. While the old woman seethed in the momentary silence, something caught my ear—a woman gleefully reading aloud and the subsequent light laughter of a child? A child?

Before I could utter another word, Mrs. Dawes shouted, "Leave!"

A frigid wind blew under and up my coat as the heavy door flew open behind me. Milly scurried in, and the afternoon light brightened the room. Firmly, she said, "Mr. Duncan, you cannot be here."

"You cannot be here!" echoed the old woman.

Grabbing me by the arm, Milly spun me around and opened the door. She moved her mouth close to my ear and whispered, "There is nothing for you here."

"Are you sure?" I asked.

Milly frowned—but not unsympathetically. There was a mild softening to her eyes. Still, with that and her light push on my back, I exited the library. The door closed behind me—but Milly did not follow. I lingered for a moment and adjusted the position of the crutch under my arm—before gathering myself and returning to the Dawes house—to my room.

NINE

I was lying on my bed when I heard Milly return to the house. She did not immediately come to my room. Instead, she went to the kitchen and eventually emerged with what I assumed was my reheated tea.

"Drink this," she said—handing me the warm cup.

"I heard reading."

"Drink," she said firmly.

I took a sip and then repeated, "I heard reading."

"Not uncommon for a library, I'd assume," snipped the usually polite young woman.

"I heard children's laughter."

"You didn't."

"I heard children's laughter."

"Drink your tea, Mr. Duncan." She dragged one of the chairs closer to the bed and sat.

I took a tentative sip and continued to press Milly for information. "I heard children's laughter."

The young woman looked down at her feet and shook her head. "You heard *a* child's laughter."

"Correcting the teacher now, are you?"

Milly ignored my quip and said, "There is nothing in the library for *you*, Mr. Duncan."

"Are you sure, Milly?" I finished the warm drink in one long gulp and placed the cup on my lap. "Are you certain?"

She didn't answer, so I continued, "The women that go there at their appointed times day after day after day, what is there for them? What do they take from those regular, daily visits?"

"Contentment," she immediately whispered.

"Yes! That's what I've seen on their faces as they leave." I sat up straighter. "But their expressions … well … contentment? It's more than that, right?"

Milly shuffled the chair closer to the bedside. "You must never repeat any of this to Mrs. Dawes — to anyone. Swear it."

I remember shrugging. I also recall the stern, silent look she gave me. "My humble apologies. I swear it. I promise you."

Following a long, deep breath, Milly began. "The men left the village because their wives became enraptured by the library — obsessed with returning each day. It was all they lived for. Nothing else got done — their households deteriorated. Their marriages disintegrated."

"Why didn't the men destroy the library?" I wrinkled my brow. "Stop Mrs. Dawes?"

The young woman restrained a laugh before continuing, "The men became ill if they approached the library or Mrs. Dawes. They simply had enough one day—scuttling three whale ships at the mouth of the cove. Taking the fourth and sailing off. They never returned."

I shook my head in disbelief at the apparent power of the old widow and asked, "What is it that has the women so enthralled?"

"Their dead children."

"Their dead children?"

"Those lost to scarlet fever—the pestilence brought by Mr. Dawes." She noticed my expression of remembrance and continued, "When the women read books they shared with their children long ago, those children appear and interact with them. A mother's greatest dream, I suppose."

"You've witnessed this?"

"No. Never seen it first-hand. I've been told by Mrs. Dawes ..." The young woman bowed her head. "... and by the mothers. At times they are so enthralled they share their encounters with me."

I wrinkled my brow and asked, "They actually appeared to their mothers? You believe this to be true?"

Milly looked up and nodded. "I have heard the laughter—their voices—when I've been with my mistress."

"But only within that library?"

"Of course," Milly answered.

"How? How is that possible?"

"Mrs. Dawes made it so." Her look into my eyes was quite serious.

I repeated, "But how is that possible?"

The young woman's intense stare took on a more frightening aspect—the corners of her eyes began to twitch. "I only know some of the history— not every detail of the actual process. I was so young when it all started, and my mistress has only recently begun to share more bits and pieces as part of my training." Milly groaned. "After Mr. Dawes was hung, she had that tree cut down and made into lumber. A large cellar was dug where the tree's roots once spread. Mr. Dawes was buried there. The wood was mixed with other timber to build the library over that cellar. Mr. Dawes loved books and brought many from his travels up and down the coast and to foreign lands."

"And how does that relate to the women? Their dead children?" I was yet to see the connection.

Milly turned toward the window. "The ache for her husband was deep. But she also missed her daughter Rebecca dearly. She spent much time alone in the cellar here—weeks. I would hand down plates of food and cups of tea. I heard her reading aloud— murmuring, chanting. At the time, I did not understand the ancient words. Eventually, she spent more time alone in the library—and, I assume, the other cellar. I was not allowed to follow her there."

I listened intently as Milly continued to stare through the window.

"Again, I was but a young girl …" She sighed. "I remember her returning from the library one evening. Her face was so different … so serene. Peaceful. Content."

"Content," I repeated.

Nodding, Milly continued, "She was—she is—a very strong-willed woman. Strong. In that successful attempt to assuage her own grief and anger, she recognized the power of what she had done—the power she could have over the other women. The power of *that* revenge on the men."

"She contacted her husband and daughter? Is that what you are saying.?"

"I am."

I shook my head as an incongruous thought crossed my mind. "And the village's men, *they* built that place for her?"

"Yes. She manipulated their guilt—their remorse—and paid them well. She told them it would be a library for the children of Black Ledge Cove. Her voice took on an especially convincing tone—her money was plentiful." Milly grinned at the recollection of her mistress's skill. "Behind their backs, she scorned them still—cursed them still."

"Cursed them?"

That question went unanswered. Milly stood and walked to the window. She glanced towards the library and then drew closed the heavy winter drapes.

"I know not all the details. They have yet to be included in my instruction." The young woman turned and looked back at me. "And I've never been permitted to descend into the library's cellar. I also know certain books of hers are locked away that I do not know. Years ago, I caught glances of her reading them. I've not seen them since."

"You've not been curious?"

"I have profound respect for Mrs. Dawes. She took me in when I came down with the fever, and my father could not care for me. He was a weak man—he left the island before I recovered. I'm in debt to her for so much."

"Understandable. Still, you've not been curious?"

Milly held up her hand and turned back to me. "I only know that she persuaded the women to bring and leave books they had shared with their children when they had been alive—to *seed* the library. I also believe she convinced them of the therapeutic effects of reading outside their homes—how it helped her heal and soothed her grief and anger."

"It cannot be as simple as that—as easy as reading the books in that building. There must be more."

Milly nodded and then returned to the chair near the bed. She sat and looked into my eyes before lowering her head and her voice. "There is. Surely, there is more. But my mistress has not seen fit to share that knowledge or that art with me as freely as she has shared others."

"Like the mixing and brewing of teas?" I quipped.

"Yes." Milly looked up—her eyes narrowed. "And the broader ancient arts of healing. She's taught me much of the old ways—to read the elder letters and words. It's not uncommon for midwives to be acquainted with much more than birthing children."

"Healing? Midwifery? Milly, surely you know there's more to this than that."

The young woman smiled. Or was that the hint of a sneer? "There are other things—what some might call the *darker* arts—Mrs. Dawes insists will require a more mature nature on my part."

I took a deep breath and asked, "Because you may not yet have the strength to steel yourself against your own spells? Because you may not yet have the restraint that has allowed her to moderate her own use of the library?"

Again, Milly nodded before casting her eyes downward. "Yes. And because I have yet to have all the necessary life experiences."

At that moment, she stood and slid the chair back to the window. After marching to the doorway, she paused, wide-eyed, and whispered, "Remember, Mr. Duncan, do not speak a word of what I've divulged."

"Yes. I remember. I promise."

It was an easy oath to keep. To whom would I speak? Mrs. Dawes? I had no desire to cross her and feel the potential wrath of her sorcery. The nearly catatonic women I occasionally passed in the village? It was difficult to detect if they even noticed my presence. No. Milly was my only confidante.

***

We were nearly finished with the evening meal before Mrs. Dawes uttered a word in my direction.

"There is nothing for you there, Mr. Duncan. The library remains off-limits." Her raspy voice grew firmer as she continued, "Remember that you are an unwelcome guest here. Unfamiliar with our ways. And that you will be leaving at the first opportunity."

"Yes, ma'am—I shall be bidding Black Ledge Cove adieu upon the vernal equinox. Please accept my apologies and appreciation for all you've done to heal my cursed affliction. I know my presence has been an unwelcome distraction." I did my best to sound contrite. "I will tend to the sheep as requested. And if there are other chores with which I may be of assistance during my brief residence here, please do not hesitate to ask."

"Very well." Mrs. Dawes returned her attention to the nearly empty bowl of stew sitting before her.

I took my last bite of supper, wiped my mouth, and carefully slid back my chair.

"I shall retire for the night."

Mrs. Dawes did not look up as she repeated, "Very well."

There was no acknowledgment from Milly, and I walked quietly to my room—thinking. I could not shake the potent pull of the library—of what I had heard within those weathered walls. Nothing for me there? I could not accept that. I did not accept that.

***

In the muted lamplight, I sat alone with my letters unbundled and spread before me on the bed. Door closed, I sobbed silently as I read the last words I had received from my beloved Cynthia. But even in my newly sober state, my mind could not recall those final weeks and days in Baltimore with any greater clarity. I still could not remember what words I had sent her or her father and how. Telegram? Letter? Honestly, I could not recall if anything was sent to her specifically. In that moment, I accepted that those memories would remain forever muddled.

Turning that last letter over in my trembling hands, I whispered, "Forgive me, Cynthia."

Was there another way to ensure her safety — to confirm that she still awaited my return? Surely what I had heard in that library conflicted with all I held dear — the logic and science of my progressive and liberal education. No. No — I could not discredit that which I had not fully investigated — that with which I had not experimented.

I neatly stacked the letters on the side table, slid further under the bed covers, and closed my eyes. Lying there, I resolved to lay my heart open for Milly. I endeavored to imagine that scene — the props, the needed words, and tears — the accompanying pain. The pain.

TEN

It was mid-afternoon the following day when Milly strode into my room and said, "I thought you might like some afternoon tea, Mr. Duncan."

I was sitting on the bed amongst my letters and turned my tear-streaked face to meet her bright, blue eyes. Her smile vanished as she presented me with a steaming cup. "Are you — ?"

"Thank you." I returned a weak smile, sipped, and remarked, "This tastes different."

"It is," confirmed Milly as she moved to retrieve one of the chairs and sit closer to the bed. After sitting, she whispered, "Are you not well?"

"I'm —" The hand holding the tea began to tremble. Milly reached out, steadied the cup, and tipped it into my mouth.

"This will help, Mr. Duncan."

"Thomas," I replied—already feeling what I assumed were the positive effects of the new tea.

Leaning closer, she whispered, "Yes, Thomas."

I caught the slightest aroma—a somewhat familiar and pleasing scent. I closed my eyes and smiled weakly. My mind drifted back to that moment in Brunswick when Cynthia had gifted me *Leaves of Grass*—when she had leaned in and whispered, "I'll always be with you in these pages and in your heart." We read several poems together before I departed for the war. It was a heartfelt moment. I lifted her last letter from the bed to my nose—again, a recognizable aroma.

With that deep and meaningful recollection, the tears flowed, and I finally told Milly of the cowardly letter I'd sent to my beloved while adrift and lost in my insecurity. I told her of Cynthia's heart-breaking reply. I told her of my uncertainties and the depths of my intoxication when I had tried to communicate with her and her father. I cursed the depravity of my dependence on that vile medicine.

"You know, beyond the quarterly supply ship, we have no contact with the outside, Thomas." Milly again reached over to help me tip tea into my mouth. "Even in emergencies. We take care of our own."

"Yes. Yes." I could feel the soothing effects of the tea—a warmth spreading from my core to the surface of my skin. "You take care of your own by allowing contact with the beyond. Those women have contact with their dead children! Perhaps I ... perhaps—"

"But your fiancée is not dead." She snatched the empty teacup from my hand. "The library will not work for you."

Even as my mania eased slightly, I could not hold back. "The letter, Milly! That cursed letter! I know not if I replied to her in earnest—or at all. I know not if she knew of my passage on the *Alomsek*. The uncertainty is consuming me. If the spell were done correctly and she *did not* appear ... her absence may provide some relief."

The young woman did not reply, so I continued, "Perhaps, perhaps, if the spell is done correctly, if everything is as it was done for the children. I have faith in your abilities, Milly. You've already done so much for me. Surely Mrs. Dawes greatly underestimates your skills."

I noted a slight blush as she replied, "And what if the answer is *not* what you wish—what if the visage of your Cynthia appears to you?

Ignoring the implication of her question, I asked, "Are there no notes in the basement here— writings that detail her spell on the women?"

"I've told you—not that I can access. Only the old books and papers she's already shared. The tools of her past midwifery. A variety of potions, powders, and herbs. Shelves of boxes and bottles. One alcove containing the pickled afterbirth and umbilical cord of all those she has delivered over the years—sealed in individual jars."

My stomach turned and soured at that last revelation, but I swallowed hard and asked, "All of the children?"

"I believe so."

"Why keep those?"

"They can be used for medicines in the future — especially against the various cancers. That's what I've been taught."

My mind was reeling. "How many jars from the births?"

"Dozens. Maybe more. It's a large alcove. She's lived here many years and delivered many babies."

I knew naught of witchcraft. I'd barely read the history of the discredited old trials in Salem. I was much more in tune with the scientific method and the use of logic I learned while at Bowdoin. "Could those remains be used in spells, Milly? Could *they* be the dark bridge that connects the women, the books, and the spirits of those children?"

She tilted her head for a moment and then grinned — but she did not speak.

I continued, "How many women are still here in Black Ledge Cove? How many use the library?

I could see Milly counting in her head before answering, "Eleven, excluding myself and Mrs. Dawes.

"Are those jars in the cellar labeled? The ones with the afterbirth? You must go into the basement and see if there are any missing. I'd wager they will correspond to the children taken by scarlet fever. Then, you must look for the notes of Mrs. Dawes — the spell she used to enchant the library and the women."

Milly put her head in her hands — thinking. In the silence, I gathered my letters back into their neat bundle.

"When you first arrived, Mrs. Dawes and I went through your belongings, Thomas." She looked up and frowned. "I know you do not carry the umbilical cord of your beloved with you."

I cringed at the thought. "No. Obviously, that was not the nature of our bond."

Pointing toward my open trunk by the window, I asked, "Perhaps the lock of hair I keep? In the volume of Whitman?" I slid to the side of the bed and dangled my leg over the side. "Might not that suffice?"

Milly shook her head. "The bond between mother and child is emotional, spiritual—and biological. The umbilical cord is a much more literal and powerful connection than a lock of hair."

"Noted." I leaned closer to the young woman. She was as bright as I had inferred. "Still …"

"Even if I can confirm your suspicions—locate the notes and the missing jars. Even then, I'm not sure I have the skill or power to modify it using a lock of hair. *That* is beyond me."

I gently held her hands and her eyes locked to mine. "I do not believe it is beyond you, Milly. You are much more capable than you let on."

She stood, set my hands in my lap, and retrieved the empty cup from the side table. "I'll get you more tea. Then I will begin my investigation of the matter."

ELEVEN

I sat on the doorsill, my leg dangling over the steep ladder that led to the dark cellar—my crutch held firmly in my right hand. Milly had rightly recommended that I not attempt to climb down and aid her in investigating Mrs. Dawes's books and jars. There was always a chance the old woman might make a surprise visit to the house, and getting caught below might meet with disaster for me. That risk was not worth satiating my curiosity in person.

I peered into the faint, orange glow and asked, "What of the jars?"

"Softly, Thomas. Keep your voice low."

Whispering firmly, I repeated, "What of the jars?"

"It's as you suspected." I could hear the clinking of her replacing jars she had moved and examined. "Those corresponding to Rebecca and the other children taken by the fever are missing."

The cellar seemed quite large as she was out of view and her footsteps on the stone floor seemed distant.

"And the missing books and notations?" I asked—my voice pushing the boundaries of what most would consider a whisper.

"If there are any, they may be in this locked cabinet. It's also in the alcove—behind a few of the jars. I'd not noticed it previously. Odd."

"What is odd, Milly?"

The lamplight and her voice moved closer to the ladder. "This old, black lacquer cabinet seems to be of the same make as the one in the sitting room adjacent to the kitchen. I wonder …"

"What do you wonder?"

The orange glow dulled, then disappeared. There was no answer from the pitch black of the cellar.

"Goodness!"

Startled, I nearly tumbled into the dark pit as Milly suddenly appeared at the foot of the ladder. After a deep breath and a moment of recovery, I repeated my question, "What do you wonder?"

"We must be alert and cautious." The serious young woman put her hands on the side railing and looked up sternly. "I must prepare the midday meal. Return to your room, and I'll bring you some tea."

"Milly." I implored.

"We must be cautious." She set her right foot on the bottom rung. "Now, up with you, Thomas."

I pulled myself up with the crutch and moved off down the hallway. Milly climbed out of the cellar, closed the heavy door, and walked into the kitchen. I watched from the shadows as she put on a kettle for tea. From inside one of the cabinets, she retrieved a ring of keys. Silently stepping forward, I watched as she moved into the sitting room. I could see nothing but faintly heard the insertion and turning of a key — the click of a lock. Fearing her discovery of my spying upon her return to the kitchen, I quietly slipped back to my room.

***

"Tea, Thomas?"

I was sitting in my chair, staring out the window, as Milly entered my room. She offered me the warm cup and sat in the adjacent chair.

After taking a long sip, I sighed — as the calm this particular mixture brought was pleasingly familiar. "Thank you."

Milly stared out into the thickening fog. "Following the midday meal and my afternoon chores, I shall again descend to the cellar. The cabinet in the sitting room is most likely of the same manufacture as the one in the cellar alcove."

"And you have access to that key?"

"I know where it is kept, yes."

"Then I shall join you later and keep watch for the Widow Dawes."

"No." She turned her head from the window. "You're to stay here. I have reason to be in the cellar —

you do not. If I am caught, it is of little consequence. If you are caught … Please, just watch from the window."

Her seriousness was evident in the tension on her face. And, as her assistance was necessary to my plan, I did not protest—I nodded.

Milly returned the gesture and let a small, crooked smile break through. "I'll bring your tea before supper and inform you of any discoveries."

"Very well."

The young woman stood and exited the room—leaving me with my tea, the window, and a curious sense of serenity.

***

For the first time in some days, the stump of my right leg throbbed. It was subtle yet persistent enough to distract me from the section of *Walden* I had been trying to read and interpret after the midday meal. I rocked slightly in my chair as I watched two women exchange places in the library.

"Thomas!"

Milly strode into the room and to my side.

With slightly trembling hands, I accepted the fresh cup of tea she offered and drank deeply.

After sitting, Milly laid a gentle hand on my knee. Her glance moved to my open trunk and then back to my eyes. "I shall need that lock of hair, Thomas."

"You found her notes. The spell? The needed old books?"

"It was all within the cabinet in the alcove."

"And you believe you can modify it for my needs?"

She nodded confidently. "I do."

"May I see the notes?"

"The papers are back in their place." Milly frowned and continued, "With the time I have available, it will take me some days to amend the words and the mixture. Then, I must access the library cellar—"

"Good." I took another long drink and finished off the tea. My hands were steady now as I handed back the empty cup with a smile. "Very good."

"Thomas, I must warn you again. The connection via the hair may not be strong enough to provide you with an answer."

"Even with your learned modifications?"

"I offer no guarantees."

"I have faith in your abilities—your desire to put my anxieties to rest."

"Yes." Milly sighed and nodded. "The lock of hair?"

Shifting to the edge of my chair, I leaned over and retrieved the Whitman from my trunk. Carefully, I withdrew the ribbon-wrapped lock of ash-brown hair and handed it to the young woman. "It's all I have of her."

"No." Milly stood and gently slid the hair into her apron pocket. "You obviously hold much more in your heart."

With that insight, she left. I glanced down at the open book in my lap. It took a moment for the words on the page to become clear, but when they did, I began to read:

> *This is the female form,*
> *A divine nimbus exhales from it from head to foot,*
> *It attracts with fierce undeniable attraction,*
> *I am drawn by its breath as if I were no more than a helpless vapor, all falls aside but myself and it …*

Breath? Vapor?

Closing my eyes, I inhaled deeply. A faint, lingering scent—a perfume—filled my nose and tugged at deep, dreamy recollections. A large house outside of Brunswick. A secluded nook in a well-maintained garden. A bench for two. The gift of a book and …? A small bottle of her favorite fragrance? Reflexively, my lips whispered, "Cynthia."

TWELVE

Over the next three days, besides my tending to the sheep or visiting the outside privy, I kept largely to my room—reading my books, drinking my tea, and watching the comings and goings at the library. Milly was busy—completing her normal chores and working on the spell in the cellar.

Upon my return from the privy on that third afternoon, I startled Milly in the kitchen as she was preparing my tea. In that surprisingly tense moment, I glimpsed her slip something from the countertop to her apron pocket before turning to face me.

"I'll have your tea momentarily, Thomas," she said as the water in the kettle began to roil.

I nodded and feigned walking to my room. Instead, I quietly shuffled down the side hall to peek in the other entrance to the sitting room. There, I saw

Milly extract a small bottle from her apron, place it into the black lacquer cabinet, and lock the closed door. As she returned to the kitchen, I snuck back to my room.

Waiting impatiently by the window, a few beads of sweat formed on my forehead. That small bottle I had just seen Milly handling was most familiar. There was a tingling in the stump of my right leg as I stood propped on my crutch and looked out at the swirling snow. An acidic emptiness gnawed at the pit of my stomach.

"Tea, Thomas."

Pivoting, I saw Milly grinning. I wiped my damp brow and sat.

She handed me the cup and took a seat.

"How … how goes your progress?" I stammered a bit as I warily sipped the hot brew.

"My interpretations and modifications are complete." Milly stared out the window. The library was barely visible through the thick, falling snow. "This will be a good evening to go to the library and make the needed preparations. Once Mrs. Dawes is fast asleep—"

"I shall follow you with my book. With the book Cynthia and I read together."

"No. Not tonight." Milly glanced at the cup and nodded. I drank more, and she continued, "But I shall require the book for my preparations."

As a hazy serenity began settling over me, I retrieved *Leaves of Grass* from my trunk and handed it to her. "When?"

"Patience, Thomas." Milly ran a finger over the edges of the book. Leaning closer, she whispered, "You know we must be cautious. Crossing Mrs. Dawes … well … we must not be discovered."

At that moment, I frowned—not just at the request for patience but because something seemed subtly different about Milly's appearance. Her complexion? Her eyes? Her …? As she leaned back, my line of inquiry was interrupted when I again caught the hint of a familiar, pleasant fragrance. That aroma evoked a reflexive smile, and I nodded. "Of course. Patience."

I drained the cup and handed it to Milly. She stood and started towards the hallway.

"And my book?"

"It will need to remain in the library." Milly turned back and whispered, "It will be well hidden amongst the others."

She said not another word as she exited, and I, again, was alone with my thoughts.

***

Either that evening's stew was unremarkable, or my somewhat muddled mind was preoccupied with Milly's plan—and the potential of having my most nagging question answered. I remembered nothing of my supper with Mrs. Dawes. I recall only retiring to my room and Milly again bringing me tea.

"May you rest easy and sleep well tonight, Thomas."

"Thank you. But it will not be easy." I set the cup on the windowsill and grasped her forearm. Looking her in the eye, I whispered firmly, "You have the power and the ability, Milly. I know you do. I believe it."

Her wide eyes softened, and I released my hand. A small smile bent her mouth, and she tucked a small tuft of ash-brown hair back into her bonnet before she turned and closed the heavy winter drapes. Brown hair? I recalled it being blonde. Perhaps a misremembrance formed during the madness of my withdrawal? No matter, it happily reminded me of my beloved.

Milly's dress brushed my shoulder on her way to the door. She paused and quietly said, "Your confidence in me … it means a great deal. Thank you, Thomas."

With that, she was gone, and I was again left with that light and pleasing scent in the air. This time the perfume not only produced a whisper of a name— *Cynthia*—but conjured a nearly corporeal image of her person in my thoughts.

***

It was well after the ten o'clock hour when I heard Milly leave the house. I stopped reading and pulled the curtain aside slightly. Peeking into the dark and squinting, I saw a hunched shadow disappear amidst the still-falling snow. The library itself was obscured by the harsh winter weather. I had long finished that last cup of tea she had brought, and my sense of calm was waning. Focus eluded me, so I placed my volume of *Walden* back in my trunk.

There, I saw that my bundle of letters had slipped down along one side and that my clothing was disturbed. I withdrew the letters and set them on the other chair. My eyes returned to the lightly rumpled pile of clothing. Was something missing? Perhaps Milly had taken something to launder?

I prodded and lifted and realized what had been removed—the uniform trousers I had been wearing when I lost my leg in that cornfield. My vision narrowed—the edges greying and closing in. Sweat ran down my back. Why had I kept those shredded and blood-soaked pants? Or was my memory failing me yet again?

My trembling hand poked at some other items in my trunk—*Moby Dick*, the *Iliad*, a knitted scarf. There was a writing set in a carved wooden box that I'd received upon graduation from Bowdoin. But those tattered trousers? The small ampule of my beloved's perfume? Had I lost that in my thoughtlessness? And where was my Whitman? Had I packed it? Had I lost it here, in Baltimore, or near Antietam? Cynthia would be furious. What other keepsakes of hers had I misplaced in my various stupors, rants, or rages?

I rocked in the chair and sobbed. My vision blurred, and my eyelids grew heavy. I remember nothing more of that evening.

THIRTEEN

"Oh! Thomas!"

A muffled shuffle of footsteps ended near where I lay in a heap on the floor under the window. I stirred and barely opened my swollen, bleary eyes. The beautiful young woman hovering over me tilted her head and frowned with concern.

"I must get you up and ready for breakfast."

Milly. Yes, the beautiful young woman speaking was Milly.

"Perhaps some tea?" I muttered. Was I half joking or half pleading? I could not recall.

She scoffed and said, "Up, Thomas."

Shifting and levering up to sit against the wall, I cleared my throat and croaked, "I … I must go to the library tonight."

"Keep your voice down." There was a heavy sigh as Milly bent closer and whispered, "If it will get you up to the table with Mrs. Dawes, if it will get you to the winter barn to tend to the sheep. Yes, we can go to the library tonight."

That answer buoyed my spirit, and I was revitalized just enough to pull myself up without my crutch. I looked down at my soiled, damp trousers and a shiver ran through my body. Tears welled in my bloodshot eyes, and I sighed, thinking I should wash up and change my clothes.

Milly sniffed the acrid air, nodded, and glanced at the pitcher and basin on the chest of drawers. "Be thorough about it and join us in the kitchen."

Ignoring last night's inability to control my bodily functions, I enthusiastically washed and changed into fresh clothes. Tonight, my questions would be answered—I would know the fate of my beloved.

***

Breakfast was uneventful—Mrs. Dawes, her typically silent, stoic self. A somewhat different morning brew both eased my thoughts and invigorated my body.

I could have made quick work of feeding the sheep and replenishing their water, but as I stared into the hay stall, my mind drifted elsewhere. The library. Cynthia. So, instead of finishing my chores quickly, I dithered and returned to the house just before the midday meal.

I shuffled into the kitchen and struggled to sit and join the others at the table without trembling.

"Are you not well, Mr. Duncan?" asked the Widow Dawes as she looked up from her bowl of broth.

"Fine." I lied as a trickle of sweat ran down my back.

"I trust you did not venture beyond the winter barn again."

For a moment, I was taken aback. Apparently, she had somehow found out about my exploration and subsequent fall. "I did not. I moved more hay into the ground-level stall. The task required more time and effort than I anticipated."

The older woman just grunted and returned to her meal. I dipped the dark bread into my broth and took a hearty bite. Milly turned my way and asked, "Tea?"

My mouth still full, I grinned and nodded. She stood and poured the steaming mixture from the nearby teapot into my cup. It was hot, but I managed a long draw. A recognizable stillness settled over me, and I stared down into the golden liquid—wondering what ingredients she had been using of late. Yet, after a few more sips, the potential answer to that question rapidly evaporated from my mind.

***

Later, following the evening meal, Milly quietly came into my room. Her only whispered words were: "Be ready at the ten o'clock hour." She left behind a fresh cup of tea and the hint of that pleasingly familiar aroma.

Until then, my afternoon and evening had been typical—reading, resting, and observing the comings and goings at the library. I'd not obsessed over what was to come. But that scent. I could not get that fragrance out of my nose or my mind. After nearly draining my cup in one gulp, I retrieved the bundle of letters from my trunk. Holding them to my nose, I inhaled. Cynthia.

***

Milly arrived just after ten o'clock and began assisting me with my greatcoat.

I whispered, "Mrs. Dawes?"

"She will sleep quite well this evening—deep."

"A special tea for her?" I asked.

Milly grinned briefly before her expression turned serious. "Now, there is little light this night, and we must not use the lantern until we are inside the library. So—"

"So, I must be deliberate with my footing and my crutch."

Milly nodded and put an arm around my back. "And mind my guidance."

"Yes."

***

I was pleased to close the heavy door of the library behind us. The slow pace across the unevenly frozen ground in brisk, damp winds had chilled me to the bone—even in my heavy overcoat. Upon entering, Milly lit the oil lamp and set it on the desk where Mrs. Dawes typically sat. The image of her standing there harshly rebuking me returned, and I gasped at that haunting memory.

"Fear not, Thomas." There was a gentle hand on my shoulder. "She will not interrupt us."

"Yes. Thank you."

The young woman lit a candle and whispered, "Now, follow me."

To call the library a labyrinth would be an understatement. The darkness—because of the unusual lack of windows—was absolute but for the weak, orange glow of the candle. Our shadows did a disturbing dance on the wood-paneled walls as we walked the short and oddly angled hallways. The many small and intimate reading rooms were barely noticeable. With each of our steps, the floorboards creaked out of time with the more rhythmic groaning of the walls as the building was buffeted by steady, cold winds.

Finally, we stopped and entered one of those dark nooks. The flickering candlelight revealed little more than walls lined with shadowy bookshelves. Milly found and lit the room's oil lamp. Its stronger glow revealed two soft reading chairs and a small table. Upon the table lay my volume of *Leaves of Grass*.

My head whip-turned to Milly. She nodded and then motioned towards the chair with one hand.

I removed my coat, sat, set my crutch to the side, and stared at the book.

"I suggest you start with one of the poems you read together."

For a moment, I was lost—my eyes unfocused. "We read it all together."

"Then I suggest trying one of the poems that stirred you both—left you breathless for more to share."

I opened the book and looked up as Milly took a step back.

"I will be nearby, Thomas."

With that, Milly retreated into the hallway—into the darkness—and extinguished her candle.

I was alone with my breath, my heartbeat, and Whitman. I thumbed through the pages for what seemed an eternity, settled back at the very beginning, and began to read *Song of Myself*.

Eleven stanzas I read aloud. Nothing. I paused and looked around. The flicker of the lamp flame was all I saw. The groaning of the building's bones was all I heard. No apparition. No Cynthia. Feeling a sense of relief, my eyes widened, the corners of my mouth turned up, and I whispered, "She's alive. My beloved must be alive and waiting—"

But my revelry—such as it was—was interrupted when I heard Milly step into the doorway and firmly say, "According to the notes of Mrs. Dawes, it takes longer with the first reading. Try reading more or another poem to be certain. Patience, Thomas."

After the young woman again quietly backed into the hallway, I inhaled deeply—now noting the presence of that oddly familiar and pleasing perfume.

I exhaled. Cynthia. Tears formed in my eyes as I began back at the beginning of the poem. I read with a fervor that would have pleased my beloved.

> *I celebrate myself, and sing myself,*
> *And what I assume you shall assume,*
> *For every atom belonging to me as good belongs to you.*

The orange glow of the lantern pulsed—momentarily brightening and dimming. I repeated the last line with even more passion.

> *For every atom belonging to me as good belongs to you.*

The lantern continued to pulse, and I read the line one more time.

> *For every atom belonging to me as good belongs to you.*

The variations ceased, and the light remained dimmer. Behind the vacant chair, a faintly glowing white haze swirled until it began taking form—the beautiful silhouette of my beloved.

"Cynthia?"

There was no reply. I grasped my crutch and stood. The specter smoothly moved a step back. Still, I could see it was her. It was her! My excitement quickly turned to dread—and the shaking in my leg took over my entire body. I collapsed in a heap back into the chair.

At that moment, the apparition disappeared. The trembling turned to spasms as I began to sob and cry out, "Gone! She's gone! I killed her. Cynthia! I—"

"I'm here, Thomas. I'm here for you."

"Cynthia?" In my delirium, I could not discern the voice. I only knew it was feminine and calming.

One hand was firmly on my shoulder, and the other offered something in a white cup. "Drink, Thomas."

"Dead. Dead. Dead. Because of me and my—"

"Drink, Thomas." The kind young woman's voice was a bit firmer.

I sipped the warm tea as the rim met my quivering lips.

"Finish it all, and then I will take you home— back to your room."

That was all I remember of that evening—my first encounter in the library.

FOURTEEN

Three sharp raps on the doorframe startled me awake. I quickly sat up in bed and moaned.

"Breakfast shortly, Thomas." It was all I heard of Milly before she disappeared down the hallway.

There was a mild but persistent throbbing in my temples and the stump of my right leg as I stood. Staring through the mirror over the washbasin, I replayed what I could recall of the scene in the library. For the moment, I managed to restrain my tears—to bury my despair.

That morning's meal was quiet. The high winds had subsided, but the heavy snowfall continued and grayed the dawn more than was usual in Black Ledge Cove.

After clearing away my empty bowl and eyeing my cup, Milly finally broke the silence. "Thomas, would you like more tea before you head to the winter barn?"

"Please." My eyes ached as they moved to meet hers. "That would be most welcome."

"I shall bring it to your room."

I nodded to the young woman, then to the seemingly indifferent Mrs. Dawes, and left the kitchen.

***

Half an hour or so later, Milly walked into the room, nodded at the letters strewn on my bed, and opened her mouth to speak. But I immediately stood and interrupted, "I must see her again, talk to her, explain to her, ask for forgiveness. I must see her again."

The young woman set a cup on my side table and pursed her lips. "We can go tonight."

"At the ten o'clock hour?" I asked.

"The same." Milly took a step back and glanced at the steaming tea before turning her eyes to me. "I think this is a promising idea to help you heal. Just hold yourself together until then, Thomas."

I struggled to produce a weak grin before picking up and drinking from my teacup. "I will."

***

Much in the reading room was the same as the previous night, except Milly poured a cup of tea from a large flask and bade me drink it before I started my reading. I was already shaking at the thought of the coming encounter and readily acquiesced — draining the cup in one long draw.

Milly refilled my cup, withdrew from the room, and extinguished her candle. There was a light rustling while she removed her long, heavy coat — then, silence. As I took a deep breath to focus my mind, I smelled that familiar perfume. The aroma was stronger and already wafting throughout the room — a favorable sign?

Opening the book to *Song of Myself*, I began reading. As before, I read many pages with no results. I returned to the one line that seemed to evoke a response on that prior evening and repeated it with a feverish yearning.

> *For every atom belonging to me as good belongs to you.*
> *For every atom belonging to me as good belongs to you.*
> *For every atom belonging to me …*

Finally, the oil lamp's flame pulsed and dimmed. The white swirl of an apparition appeared near the doorway and slowly began to take form.

Even while still sitting, my hands and limbs began to tremble. Perspiration beaded on my brow and back. Tears welled in my eyes. My quivering lips tried to form words, but nothing came. I shakily raised the teacup to my mouth and drank.

The bright, ethereal whiteness gradually became more defined. The folds of a yellow dress, crossed arms, long, graceful fingers. I glanced at the empty teacup and back to Cynthia. It was surely her.

The face was yet to manifest in detail, but I already knew.

"Cynthia!"

There was a whisp of sound but no words. The lamplight pulsed and dimmed so as to nearly extinguish itself. In that instant, my beloved's form seemed to solidify — to become corporeal.

My body trembled as I braced on my crutch and stood. It took but four steps to stand directly in front of Cynthia. Through the still hazy aura, I could discern her sad blue eyes, ash brown hair, her slight smile.

"Cynthia." Tears ran down my cheeks and into my beard. "My beloved, I humbly ask your forgiveness. I was ... I—"

Reaching out and stepping forward, she pulled me into a firm embrace. I know not how long we held each other before I could feel her breath near my ear — her increasingly intense inhalations and exhalations — or sense the warmth of her body.

"I love you, Thomas," she whispered. "I will always be yours."

I gently slipped back while still embracing — trying to focus on the still somewhat ethereal face of my beloved.

"How?" I could feel the sweat begin to bead on my back and brow again. "How can this be? You're dead. The victim of my weakness. How can you forgive me? Can you ever forgive me?"

"There is nothing to forgive. We *will* be together."

"But how? How? Only the dead visit this library? You are the victim of my depravity. Oh, my Cynthia—"

A gentle hand brushed my face. "Close your eyes, my love. For I must go."

I complied, and it was then that she kissed me.

"Stay," I implored. "Stay with me."

"Please, beloved, Thomas. For now, I must go." Cynthia pulled me closer and whispered in my ear. "Close your eyes again. Keep them closed. Know that I will be with you again."

She stepped back, and her warmth—and my warmth—immediately disappeared. The sudden chill of my perspiration elicited the return of my shivering—breaking the spell of the moment. I opened my eyes, and the corporeal form was gone—even the apparition was no more. There was nothing—no one.

In the dim lamplight, I stumbled backward and collapsed into the chair. Through bleary eyes, I noticed the full teacup on the table. Had I not consumed it all earlier? Next to it now sat a tempting, small bottle.

I rocked as my aching eyes moved from teacup to bottle and back. I drained the cup and stared at the open book of Whitman also on the table. Could I conjure her again? If I read the passage again, would Cynthia return? Would she speak with me again? Embrace me? Kiss me?

My head throbbed to the beat of my ranting thoughts. On the table, I saw guaranteed relief. I snatched and emptied that familiar bottle and quickly slipped into a haze of weak orange lamplight and swirling half-memories.

FIFTEEN

"Mr. Duncan, are you not well?" asked Mrs. Dawes at the breakfast table. I was sure she had noticed the light sweat on my forehead.

I was not myself—having no recollection of the previous evening following Cynthia's departure from the library. I could only assume that Milly had guided me back to the house and my room. "Sleep eluded me for most of last night, ma'am."

Milly looked to her mistress and then back to me. "Perhaps I should tend to the sheep this morning, Mr. Duncan."

I sighed.

Mrs. Dawes shook her head but said, "Very well. Rest today. Return to the sheep tomorrow. I'll see that Milly brings you something to aid in your recovery."

***

"As directed by Mrs. Dawes."

Milly entered my room and set a teacup on my side table.

"The only thing I really want — need — is to return to the library." Ignoring the steaming tea, I continued, "Last night ... last night ... I held my beloved and ... and ... she forgave my weakness. She ..."

The young woman stepped closer and leaned toward the bed. "I think it best that we abstain from using the library for a couple of days. I do not want Mrs. Dawes growing suspicious or the two of us getting careless in — "

"But I must hold Cynthia again." I shifted closer to the edge of the bed and reached towards Milly with my nearest, trembling hand. She backed away, and I pleaded, "Please, I can think of nothing else. Please, I must — "

"Two days, Thomas."

With that, the young woman abruptly exited. I took a deep breath to steel myself against the likely physical and emotional torment of the next two days, but a light scent tickled my nostrils and disrupted my brief resolve. Cynthia?

I know not how long I sat on the bed rocking — my unfocused eyes drifting from my trunk to the window to the library. I only know that eventually, I remembered the tea on the side table. Though it had cooled and become considerably less appealing, I emptied the cup, and, in moments, my rampaging thoughts began to quiet.

***

It had been an unusual day. Milly did not bring my usual cup of tea prior to the midday meal or later in the afternoon. She seemed oddly absent from the house except for mealtimes. I did not get the now much-needed relief of my tea except while eating — and even then, the respite from my manic thoughts seemed tenuous and more temporary.

Through my frosted window, at the seven o'clock hour, I spied Mrs. Dawes, lantern in one hand and cane in the other, struggling over the roughly frozen ground while returning to the house. The library was now empty.

I listened carefully through my cracked open door. Faint whispers. Milly and Mrs. Dawes in the kitchen. I held my breath and could barely hear the kettle's roar over the ticking clock on the dresser and the beat of my heart. It was some time before the house fell completely silent.

The minutes passed, and my thoughts raced back to my beloved. The hours passed, and my body ached to hold Cynthia once more — twice more. Forever.

Perspiration beaded on my forehead and back as I sat in bed to read that last letter again. Could I be with her forever? The stump of my right leg throbbed and burned. Could the library facilitate that permanent reunion? My eyes teared while I stared into the flickering light of my lantern. Could I persuade Mrs. Dawes to allow me to stay?

First, I needed to be sure of what I'd seen, heard, and held. I needed to return to the library and confirm Cynthia's forgiveness—be reassured of her willingness to be with me. Yet I was overcome—overwhelmed with the weakness of wavering. I was afraid to make the journey alone—of losing my footing in the snow. I was terrified of the potential catastrophic disappointment. My hands trembled as I picked up and crumbled the last correspondence from my beloved. I had to go to the library, and I had to go now.

After donning my pants, heavy woolen shirt, and overcoat, I slowly hobbled down the side hallway—conscious of quietly placing my crutch and left foot for each step. Painstakingly, I went through the sitting room to the kitchen. There, I retrieved the ring of keys I'd seen Milly use to open the black lacquer cabinet. Returning to the parlor, I lowered myself to the floor and stared at the keyhole. I knew what was behind that door—even though I'd never formed the words in my mind. I knew the Pandora's Box I was potentially opening. Still, I turned the key and revealed a familiar wooden box stenciled with comforting words: *Tallac & Sons, Laudanum.*

My hands trembled, but I managed to slide aside the lid and withdraw six precious bottles—slipping them into the pocket of my coat. Still, I sat frozen and stared at the crate. Many bottles were missing. More than six. Was it confirmation of what I'd been suspecting? Or had I been secretly coming to the cabinet myself these last few days? It was unlikely, but I was unsure. Instead of losing myself in the paralysis of rumination, I picked out one more bottle, removed the cork, and drank.

It provided all the courage I needed. Bracing myself on the cabinet, I stood and retraced my steps — returning the keyring and using the side hallway. Had I locked the cabinet? Did I put the now empty bottle back? I didn't care. I focused on the immediate tasks — getting quietly out the front door, surviving the bitter and treacherous walk to the library, and reuniting with my fiancée.

SIXTEEN

A welcome medicinal haze fell over me as I hobbled my way through the library's dark maze to the same reading room I'd used the previous two nights. After setting down the lamp, I emptied my pockets of the bottles of opium I had recovered. Removing my coat, I threw it over the back of my chair and sat. Whitman? Where was my volume of *Leaves of Grass*? Burning eyes darted across the table, to the other chair, and along the shelves. I needed that book—but there was nothing on the table except the laudanum and lantern.

Perhaps? I lifted my overcoat and felt around my back. Success! Stuffed into the crook of the cushions was my book—*our* book. Now?

I panicked at thinking Milly's presence may be necessary for the conjuring. My left leg spasmed, and the book fell to the floor. Instead of immediately retrieving it, I reached for one of the tiny bottles on the table. Once it was drained of precious elixir, I picked up the *Leaves of Grass* and opened to *Song of Myself*.

The beads of perspiration transformed into a full sweat as I began to read that passionate bard's beautiful words. As I did the previous two nights, I read a long section of the poem before returning to the first few lines. The words slurred as the opium tonic began to course through my veins — to narrow my vision and muffle my ears. Lifting my gaze, my eyes darted around the dimly lit room — searching for the slightest swirl of an apparition, listening for a whisper, hoping for anything.

But there was nothing save the lamplight dancing across the bookshelves.

"Cynthia!" I beckoned. "Come to me, Cynthia!"

Bracing myself on my crutch, I stood on one trembling leg. I still saw nothing, and all I heard was the racing beat of my own heart. The contents of another bottle found its way into my mouth — into my thoughts. Picking up the book, I mumbled my way through the first lines of the poem — repeating the last few powerful words as I had done before. Once more, *nothing*. The Whitman slipped from my hand as I whispered, "Cynthia ... beloved, Cynthia ... why have you not returned? Have you forsaken me?"

What was different? What was missing? Milly? Something in the cellar? That pleasing perfume? All I could smell was the burning oil in the lantern and my own pungent perspiration. Nothing pleasing about that! Nothing!

Enraged, I swung my crutch and knocked the lantern flying. Crashing on the floor next to the nearby wall of books, it burst into flames. The fire quickly danced up the bookshelf and along the ceiling.

"Cynthia!" I screamed—lips quivering and dripping with drool--bloodshot eyes bulging. "Cynthia!"

Without my crutch, my left leg faltered, and I stumbled backward—collapsing on the floor next to the chair. I slobbered as I stuttered, "Oh … my … my Cyn … Cynthia … mm … my …"

"Thomas!"

A recognizable voice turned my head towards the hallway. At first, there was but a black silhouette—backlit by the glow of a lamp in the hallway.

"Oh, Thomas!"

My vision was not clear, but even under a heavy winter cloak, the beautiful yellow dress was recognizable. As she stepped closer, the strength of her perfume battled with the smell of the thickening smoke.

"Thomas. What have you done?"

My eyes burned and teared from the smoke, yet somehow, as she neared, her visage seemed clearer than the previous evening.

"You've come, Cynthia! You're back!" I pawed at the chair to try and pull myself up—but to no avail. As I rocked, she took the remaining bottles from the table and slipped them into a pocket in her coat.

"Come. Take my arm! We must leave now!"

With Milly's assistance, I clumsily fell into the chair, and she tugged my greatcoat into place. The soft touch of her gloved hand wiped the sweat from my brow, and she kissed my cheek. I could see her eyes take in the scene—the growing fire—as she whispered, "You must heed my instructions, Thomas. We will leave together now—escape this place at once."

With a strong pull from my beloved, I stood again on my wobbly left leg. She slipped my right arm over her shoulder, and we shuffled into the hallway.

***

Exiting the library, we paused. Through my tears, I could see Milly's eyes dart from house to house. Lights were visible in every home—including that of Mrs. Dawes. We stood entranced until a bitter and powerful gust of wind kicked up biting flakes of snow.

"This way, Thomas." Cynthia started to guide me through the now-blowing snow. I could feel the pitch of the icy, cobbled road—downhill. My vision was narrowed—the edges dark grey. Still, I walked. The cobbles. Milly? My left foot. The cobbles. Cynthia. My left foot.

"Quicker, Thomas. We must make for the harbor." I could hear her muffled, heavy sigh. "Make haste!"

In my medicated stupor, the going was slower and more laborious than usual, and I required a pause to rest. "Cynthia, a moment."

Frustrated and frightened, she turned—looking back towards the village and the burning library.

"She's there now—Mrs. Dawes. Outside the library. We must hurry, Thomas." Her embrace grew firmer, and we started walking at a much quicker pace. "No more rest. The others are gathering with her. They're ire—"

The young woman was cut off by a loud crash from behind. The library was beginning to collapse as it was consumed by flames.

"Quickly, my love," said Cynthia as she guided me forward.

We no longer paused and soon moved between two waterfront warehouses. As we emerged from the narrow, dark alley, my beloved's lantern revealed the dark shape of a small, open fishing boat waiting at the water's edge.

My body trembled from the exhaustive effort, and I braced myself on the gunnels of the wooden skiff. Perspiration soaked the clothing under my coat, and the pause in movement allowed the bitter cold to chill me to the bone.

"Drink these." A gloved hand holding two small bottles appeared in front of my face. From deep in my haze, I traced the arm to its source. Cynthia. She was standing in the boat—looking down. "Thomas, drink this now."

I complied and, after draining that delicious medicine, dropped the two empty bottles into the slushy, shallow water lapping at my boot. Warmth flowed through my body, yet the shivering did not abate. I rocked gently—oblivious to the noisy happenings onboard.

"We must go now. Into the boat, my beloved!" The blurry gloved hand again appeared before my heavy, teary eyes. Cynthia's voice was muffled, barely audible. "Take my arm. It will not be graceful, but we must get you onboard."

My eyes closed, and I stood frozen and fading.

"Thomas!"

The last thing I recall was two hands tightly gripping my forearms. After that, there was only the darkness of my distorted memory.

SEVENTEEN

I know neither my place nor time. Many have been my experiences with thin, smoky mists and laying somewhat askew and on my back—madly muddled have been those recollections. When am I? Where am I?

September? 1862? Wounded in that cornfield along Antietam creek?

This mist smelled of smoke, but not that tangy, metallic variety leftover from the generous expenditure of gunpowder. And there was also a gentle rocking beneath me.

December? Being rowed to the beach at Black Ledge Cove?

No. While the smoke smelled of coal, and the scent of salt water was strong, there was also an oddly pleasant, familiar fragrance.

That did not fit—even with those similar, yet jumbled, memories. So, where am I? When am I?

I strained to open my teary, swollen eyes wider—to lift or turn my heavy head--but failed. The continued, gentle rocking eased my weak mind just enough, and I slipped back into a familiar, less-conscious comfort.

***

"Ahoy!"

I struggled to move my leaden limbs under what seemed to be multiple layers of heavy, woolen blankets. The pulse in my head pounded behind my aching eyes.

"Ahoy!" The grating male voice shouted again, "Ahoy! Sir? Ma'am?"

Squinting in the bright overhead sun, I could discern two blurry silhouettes through my tears—a woman sitting upright in my boat and a large man standing above and beyond.

"Who are you? Who—" The loud voice drew nearer but was interrupted by other husky, overlapping male voices.

There was a thud as the other boat pulled alongside. I finally managed to summon the strength to lift my head and push my body into a more upright position. A few blinks cleared the tears from my eyes, and I could see several men holding the boats off while their leader moved closer.

"Sir? Ma'am? What are you doing offshore in the dead of winter in an open boat? Ship sink? I've

112

heard no such news." He shook his head. "Damned lucky to be alive. Pardon, ma'am. Who are you?"

"We are deeply appreciative of your assistance, kind sir." It was a familiar feminine voice replying. "I am Cynthia Ladd, and this is my betrothed, Thomas Wade Duncan. We were held captive on Witch's Rock."

"Cynthia," I rasped weakly, but she did not hear. "Witch's Rock ..."

"I am Mr. Caldwell, ma'am. Sailing Master. We are from the steamship *Herkimer*—en route to Albany via Providence, New York, and several other ports of call."

"Well, thank you for rescuing us, Mr. Caldwell. We would be much obliged if you would give us ..." Cynthia hesitated—considering for a moment--before continuing, "Yes, we would be obliged if you would give us passage to Albany. Of course, we can pay the required fare."

"I believe we can accommodate you, ma'am." He looked around at the other sailors onboard. Each nodded. "We also have a surgeon on board who can look after your health."

"I'm afraid that won't be necessary, Mr. Caldwell." I could see Cynthia take the hand of one of the seamen and step across to the other boat. "All we require is a berth that is warm and dry and some hot food."

"As you wish, ma'am," came the gruff reply as the Sailing Master turned to direct the retrieval and transfer of two heavily laden satchels, the mass of blankets, and myself.

***

Most of the steamship's crew or other passengers did not believe our extraordinary tale—what Cynthia told them of our marooning on that dreary island, our subsequent imprisonment in the village of Black Ledge Cove, the witchcraft of Mrs. Dawes, and the desperation of our late-night escape. When in the company of others, I repeated the story—though I'm not certain even I believed the entire account.

Prior to, and during that time on the island, my memory had been badly disjointed and jumbled by the excessive consumption of opium. It was only in the last two weeks on board the steamship—with Cynthia's patient nurturing and soothing teas—that I was finally healing from that cursed addiction and recovering some clearer fragments of memory from those weeks on the island.

I hesitated to share those piecemeal and still hazy recollections with my beloved. Even though I was still recuperating from my affliction, we had a grand time onboard the ship. We enjoyed the new, expanded volume of *Leaves of Grass* we'd purchased while in port at Providence, the interesting food, and the string quartet's evening concerts. I did not want to say anything to upset our now deepening bond or impending marriage. Instead, I'd taken to recording my incongruous thoughts in the journal we'd purchased at that same bookseller.

Now, after more than two weeks of sailing and port calls, Cynthia and I beheld the wharves and homes of Albany from the deck of the *Herkimer*. Arm in arm, we stood at the railing and started planning our new life together.

"I'd like to teach again." Tightening my grip on her arm, I added, "Perhaps have my own school in a few years."

Cynthia turned and smiled. "I'd like to further study the old texts I stole from that crone's cellar. Possibly take up midwifery."

I closed my eyes and did not respond one way or the other. But as I pulled my beloved a little closer, I realized that the inconsistent memories I had begun to document in my new journal would remain hidden within those pages--a necessary casualty of my newfound happiness.

END

AKNOWLEDGEMENTS

A special thank you goes out to my wife, Jules, for her enthusiastic reading, editing, and support of this departure from my usual subject matter.

I'm also thankful to my editor, Jennifer Sloane, for her continued fine-tuning of my work.

ABOUT THE AUTHOR

Kip Koelsch got his start writing "books" in Mrs. Cook's second grade class in Leonardo, NJ. A one-time freelance magazine writer, he currently blogs about writing, critical thinking, outdoor adventure sports, paddling and his current fiction projects. Koelsch has an undergraduate degree in Journalism and Mass Media from Rutgers University in NJ and a master's degree in Humanities and American Studies from the University of South Florida in Tampa, FL.

Koelsch's father, Arthur, inspired him to read (and write) science fiction and thrillers, and dream big. His mother, Marilyn, was his first editor, and inspired him to read extensively in multiple genres.

Koelsch lives in Dunedin, Florida, with his wife and cats.

Amazon Author Page: https://amazon.com/author/kipkoelsch
Kip Koelsch's Blog: https://kipwkoelsch.wordpress.com
Author Facebook Page:
https://www.facebook.com/KipKoelschAuthor/
Twitter: @KipAuthor
Instagram: kipauthor

Please take a moment to leave a review on this book's Amazon and/or Goodreads page when you finish reading.

Your support is greatly appreciated.

READ. IMAGINE.

Also from Kip Koelsch

MOOSE. INDIAN. A Dark Confession
(short story)

TRINARY: Three Speculative Fiction Short Stories

The Saga of the Cerulean Universe
Book One: *PIERCING THE CELESTIAL OCEAN*
Book Two: *BEYOND THE PALE BLUE SUN*
Book Three: *ON THE BRINK OF CONTINUITY*

Science-thriller Fiction
WENDALL'S LULLABY
DELPHYS RISING

Made in United States
North Haven, CT
30 April 2025

68428802R00072